Cagney & Lacey

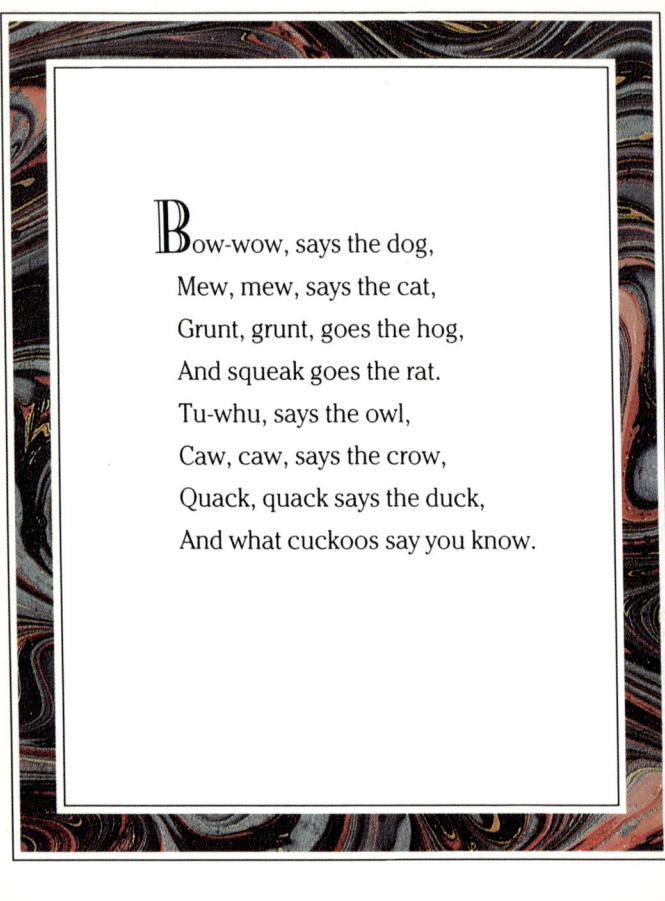

Bow-wow, says the dog,
Mew, mew, says the cat,
Grunt, grunt, goes the hog,
And squeak goes the rat.
Tu-whu, says the owl,
Caw, caw, says the crow,
Quack, quack says the duck,
And what cuckoos say you know.

Wedgwood

The child and Miss Pussy
Do play very nice;
But Pussy had much rather
Play with some mice.

Zelah

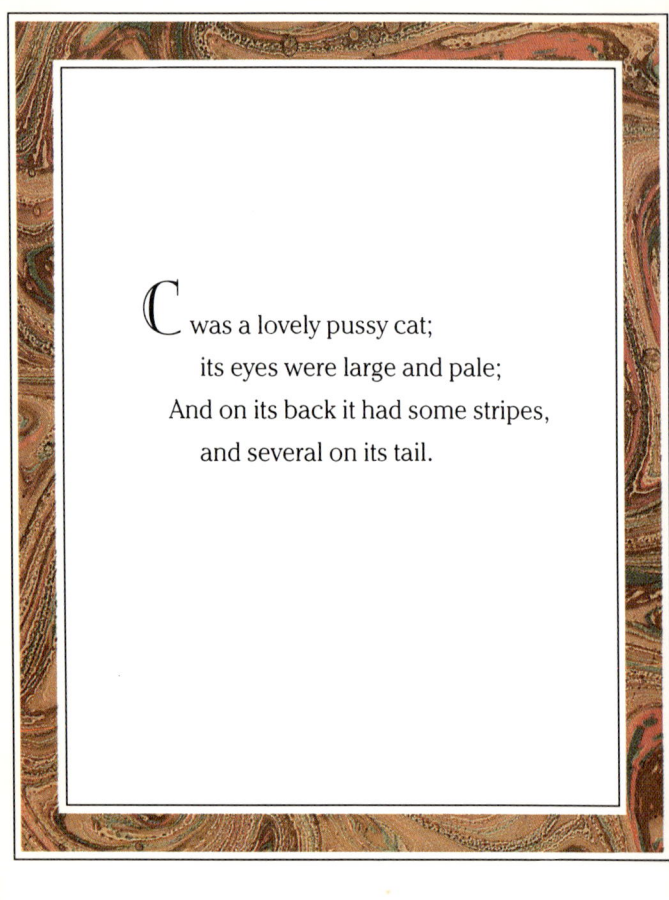

C was a lovely pussy cat;
    its eyes were large and pale;
And on its back it had some stripes,
    and several on its tail.

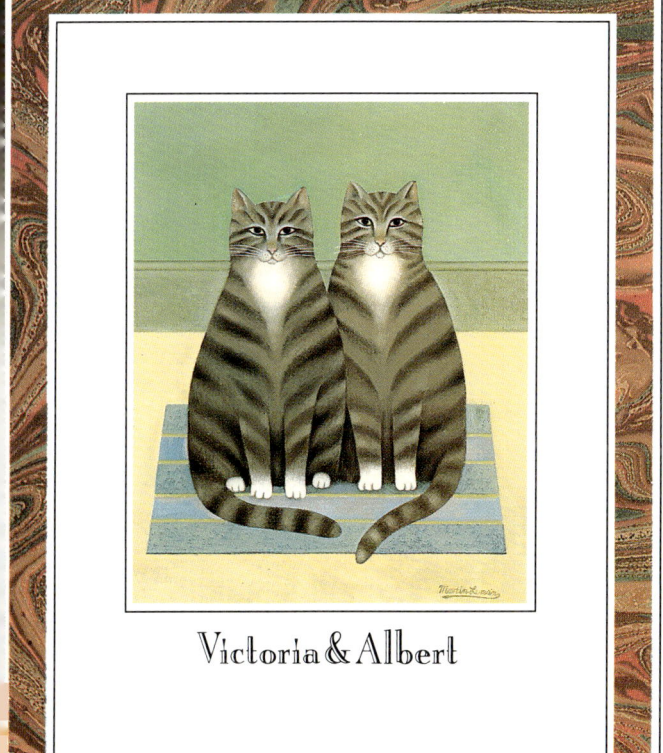

Victoria & Albert

Pussy cat, pussy cat,
  Where have you been?
I've been to London
  To look at the Queen.
Pussy cat, pussy cat,
  What did you there?
I frightened a little mouse
  Under her chair.

Shelburne

I love little pussy,
 Her coat is so warm,
And if I don't hurt her
 She'll do me no harm.
So I'll not pull her tail,
 Nor drive her away,
But pussy and I
 Very gently will play.
She shall sit by my side,
 And I'll give her some food;
And pussy will love me
 Because I am good.

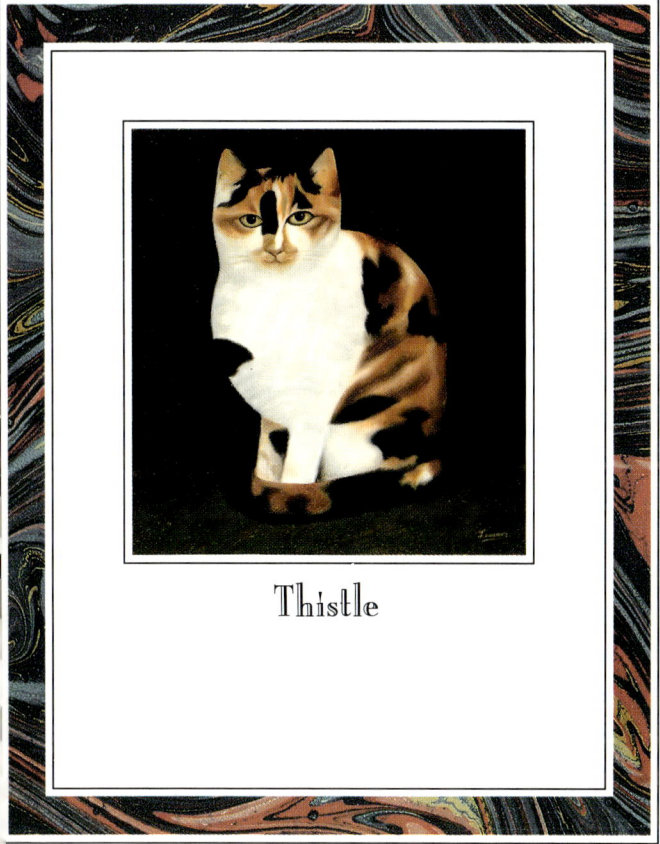

Thistle

Pussy sits beside the fire,
So pretty and so fair.
In walks the little dog,
Ah, pussy, are you there?
How do you do, Mistress Pussy?
Mistress Pussy, how do you do?
I thank you kindly, little dog,
I'm very well just now.

Kitty

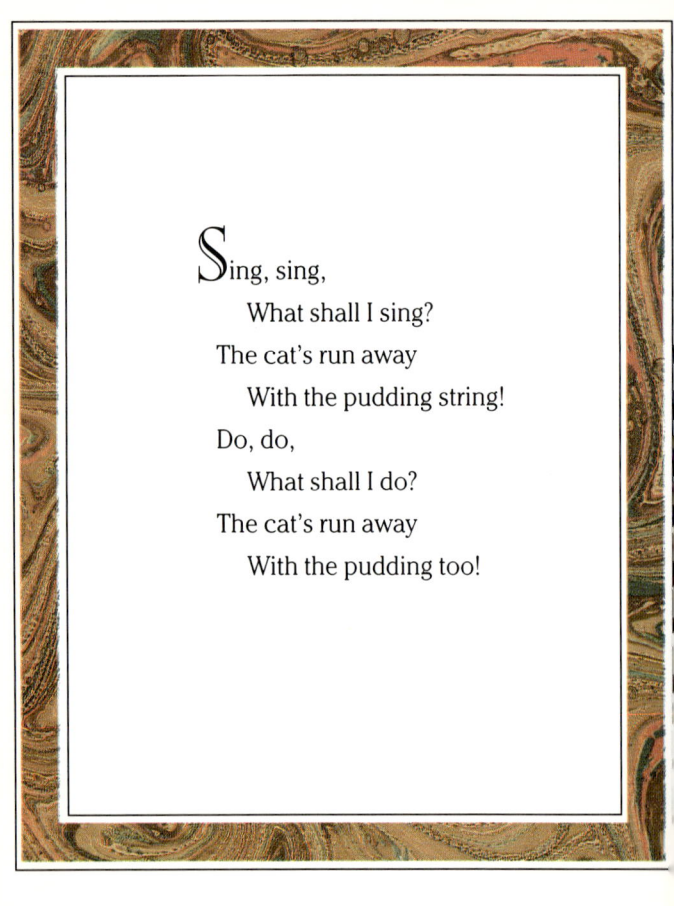

Sing, sing,
    What shall I sing?
The cat's run away
    With the pudding string!
Do, do,
    What shall I do?
The cat's run away
    With the pudding too!

Button

Great A, little a,
Bouncing B,
The cat's in the cupboard
And can't see me.

Earl Grey

Pussy-cat Mew jumped over
a coal,
And in her best petticoat
burnt a great hole.
Pussy-cat Mew shall have
no more milk
Till she has mended her
gown of silk.

Cat and Canary

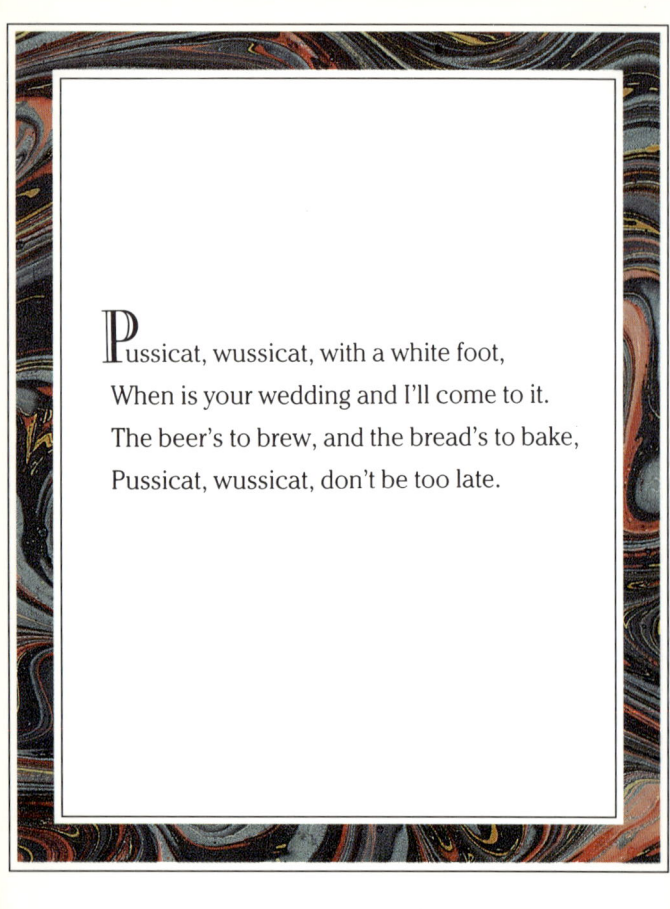

Pussicat, wussicat, with a white foot,
When is your wedding and I'll come to it.
The beer's to brew, and the bread's to bake,
Pussicat, wussicat, don't be too late.

Scruffty

Diddlety, diddlety, dumpty,
The cat ran up the plum tree;
Half a crown to fetch her down,
Diddlety, diddlety, dumpty.

May